W9-APL-881

Rainbow Fish & Friends

FOLLOW THE LEADER

TEXT BY GAIL DONOVAN
ILLUSTRATIONS BY DAVID AUSTIN CLAR STUDIO

Night Sky Books
New York • London

One afternoon Miss Cuttle announced that the class would be studying shells. "At the end of the week, we'll be taking a trip to the Oyster Beds. Angel and Puffer, since you've been there before, I'm sure you will have lots to share with us."

"Hooray!" shouted Rainbow Fish. "Field trip!"

Puffer puffed himself up. "I'll show you hundreds of pearls when we get there," he boasted.

"I can show you a Pearl right now," giggled Rosie, as she led her little sister, Pearl, up to the front of the class.

After the class settled down, Rosie swam over to Angel. "We can be partners on this field trip," suggested Rosie.

"Great idea!" said Angel.

After school, Rainbow Fish and his friends swam to the Sunken Ship. "Let's play Follow the Leader!" shouted Rosie. "Follow me! I'm the leader."

"No surprise there," said Spike, trailing after Rosie as she streaked through one of the portholes.

They passed Angel collecting shells.

"Come and join the game, Angel," called Rainbow Fish.

"No, thanks," said Angel. "I don't feel like playing Follow the Leader."

"We do play it a lot," said Rainbow Fish. "I wish we had a new game to play."

"Do you know Shark and Minnows?" Angel asked. "We used to play it all the time when I lived in the Western Waters. One fish is the shark, and all the other fish are the minnows. The minnows all try to rush past the shark, and the shark tries to tag them out."

"That sounds like fun," said Rainbow Fish. "Hey, everyone, come back here."

All the fish turned and swam back.

"What's going on?" said Rosie. "I thought we were playing Follow the Leader."

"Angel knows a new game," said Rainbow Fish.

"A new game?" muttered Rosie. "What's wrong with the one we're playing?"

"This game is called Shark and Minnows," Rainbow Fish said, and he explained the rules.

"That sounds like fun!" cried Puffer.

"I get to be the shark first," called Spike.

The next day after school Rosie shouted, "Time to play. Follow me!"

"Wait! Let's play Shark and Minnows again," said Little Blue. "This time I'm the shark."

"We played that yesterday," said Rosie. "It wasn't that much fun."

"Maybe Angel knows another game we can play," said Rainbow Fish. "Let's go ask her."

They found Angel practicing her water ballet.
"Angel, will you teach us another game?" Rainbow Fish asked.
"Okay," said Angel. "Do you know Fish, Fish, Shark?"
"What's that?" asked Little Blue.
"Make a circle and I'll show you," said Angel.

Everyone got in a circle except Rosie.

"Come on, Rosie," called Pearl.

"I don't want to play this game," said Rosie. "I'm going home."

The next morning in class, Angel swam over to Rosie. "I can't wait until the field trip. First I want to show you the famous giant oyster shell, and then you have to see the world's smallest pearl."

"Why do we always have to do everything your way?" Rosie snapped.

"What do you mean?" Angel asked, surprised.

"First you make everyone play your games, and now you expect me to follow you around the Oyster Beds," said Rosie.

"I didn't make anyone play anything. They asked me to teach them. And I thought we'd have fun at the Oyster Beds, but I guess not," she said and swished away in a huff.

Rosie jetted over to Rainbow Fish. "I can't believe how bossy Angel is," she said. "She always wants to do things her way."

"Hmm . . . sounds like another fish I know," said Rainbow Fish.

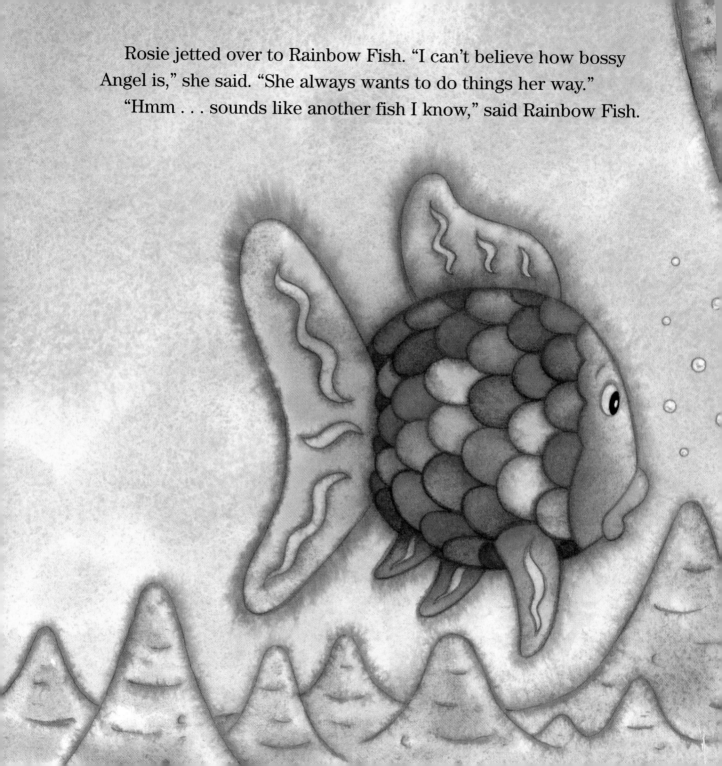

"What are you talking about?" stammered Rosie. "I take turns! Most of the time . . . well, sometimes." Rosie turned even rosier. She was quiet for a long time. Finally she said, "I think I need to talk to Angel."

Rosie found Angel and apologized. "I'm sorry I was mean," she said. "You can be the leader from now on."

"I don't always need to be the leader," said Angel. "We should all take turns."

The next morning, Miss Cuttle asked, "Is everyone ready for the field trip? Please find your partner."

Rosie raced over to Angel. "Ready, buddy?" she asked.

"Ready!" said Angel.

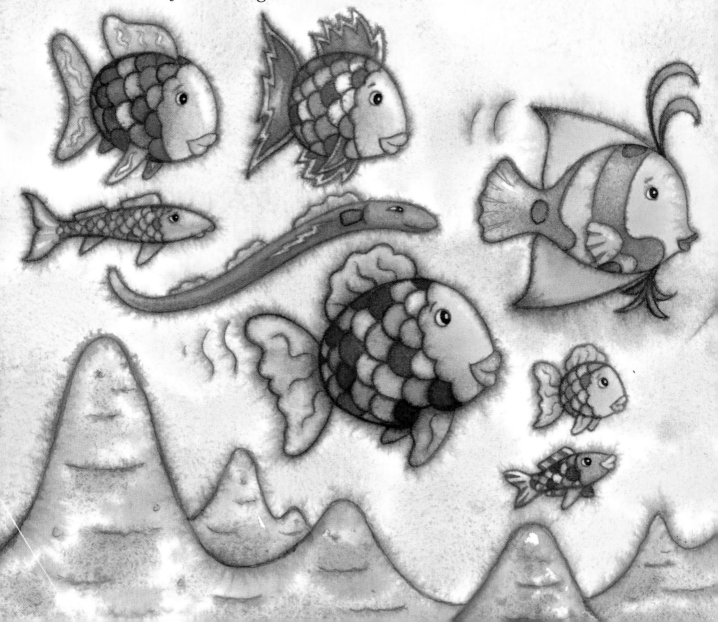

"Shall we play Follow the Leader on the way to the Oyster Beds?" asked Miss Cuttle.

Everyone in class looked at Rosie.

"I think it's Pearl's turn to be the leader," said Rosie.

"Hooray!" cheered Pearl. "Follow me!"

Rosie giggled. "But . . ."

". . . I get to be the leader on the way home."

Night Sky Books
A division of North-South Books Inc.

Copyright © 2003 by Nord-Süd Verlag AG, Gossau Zürich, Switzerland
First published in Switzerland under the title *Der Spielverderber*
English translation copyright © 2003 by Night Sky Books,
a division of North-South Books Inc., New York

All rights reserved. No part of this book may be reproduced or
utilized in any form or by any means, electronic or mechanical,
including photocopying, recording, or any information storage and
retrieval system, without permission in writing from the publisher.

First published in the United States and Canada in 2003 by
Night Sky Books, a division of North-South Books Inc.

Library of Congress Cataloging-in-Publication Data is available.

ISBN 1-59014-115-6
1 3 5 7 9 LE 10 8 6 4 2
Printed in Germany

For more information about our books, and the authors and artists
who create them, visit our web site: www.northsouth.com